'Twas the Night Before Christmas

A Visit from St. Nicholas

By Clement C. Moore

With Pictures by Jessie Willcox Smith

A HOLIDAY CLASSIC

HOUGHTON MIFFLIN HARCOURT
Boston   New York

INTRODUCTION

AMID the many celebrations last Christmas Eve, in various places by different persons, there was one, in New York City, not like any other anywhere. A company of men, women, and children went together just after the evening service in their church, and, standing around the tomb of the author of "A Visit from St. Nicholas," recited together the words of the poem which we all know so well and love so dearly.

Dr. Clement C. Moore, who wrote the poem, never expected that he would be remembered by it. If he expected to be famous at all as a writer, he thought it would be because of the Hebrew Dictionary that he wrote.

He was born in a house near Chelsea Square, New York City, in 1781; and he lived there all his life. It was a great big house, with fireplaces in it; — just the house to be living in on Christmas Eve.

Dr. Moore had children. He liked writing poetry for them even more than he liked writing a Hebrew Dictionary. He wrote a whole book of poems for them.

One year he wrote this poem, which we usually call "'T was the Night before Christmas," to give to his children for a Christmas present. They read it just after they had hung up their stockings before one of the big fireplaces in their house. Afterward, they learned it, and sometimes recited it, just as other children learn it and recite it now.

It was printed in a newspaper. Then a magazine printed it, and after a time it was printed in the school readers. Later it was printed by itself, with pictures. Then it was translated into German, French, and many other languages. It was even made into "Braille"; which is the raised printing that blind children read with their fingers. But never has it been given to us in so attractive a form as in this book. It has happened that almost all the children in the world know this poem. How few of them know any Hebrew!

Every Christmas Eve the young men studying to be ministers at the General Theological Seminary, New York City, put a holly wreath around Dr. Moore's picture, which is on the wall of their dining-room. Why? Because he gave the ground on which the General Theological Seminary stands? Because he wrote a Hebrew Dictionary? No. They do it because he was the author of "A Visit from St. Nicholas."

E. McC.

'Twas the Night before Christmas

WAS the night before Christmas, when all through

the house

Not a creature was stirring, not even a mouse;

The stockings were hung by the chimney with care

In hopes that St. Nicholas soon would be there;

HE children were nestled all snug in their beds,

While visions of sugar-plums danced in their heads;

And mamma in her kerchief, and I in my cap,

Had just settled our brains for a long winter's nap,

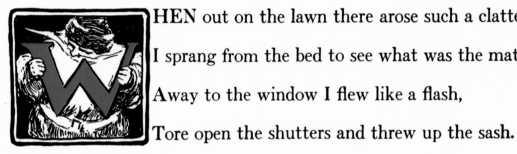

HEN out on the lawn there arose such a clatter,

I sprang from the bed to see what was the matter.

Away to the window I flew like a flash,

Tore open the shutters and threw up the sash.

HE moon on the breast of the new-fallen snow

Gave the lustre of mid-day to objects below,

When, what to my wondering eyes should appear,

But a miniature sleigh, and eight tiny reindeer,

WITH a little old driver, so lively and quick,

I knew in a moment it must be St. Nick.

More rapid than eagles his coursers they came,

And he whistled, and shouted, and called them by name;

OW, *Dasher!* now, *Dancer!* now, *Prancer* and *Vixen!*

On, *Comet!* on, *Cupid!* on, *Donder* and *Blitzen!*

To the top of the porch! to the top of the wall!

Now dash away! dash away! dash away all!''

S dry leaves that before the wild hurricane fly,

When they meet with an obstacle, mount to the sky;

So up to the house-top the coursers they flew,

With the sleigh full of **Toys**, and St. Nicholas too.

AND then, in a twinkling, I heard on the roof

The prancing and pawing of each little hoof.

As I drew in my head, and was turning around,

Down the chimney St. Nicholas came with a bound.

E was dressed all in fur, from his head to his foot,

And his clothes were all tarnished with ashes and soot;

A bundle of Toys he had flung on his back,

And he looked like a pedler just opening his pack.

IS eyes — how they twinkled! his dimples how merry!

His cheeks were like roses, his nose like a cherry!

His droll little mouth was drawn up like a bow,

And the beard of his chin was as white as the snow;

HE stump of a pipe he held tight in his teeth,

And the smoke it encircled his head like a wreath;

He had a broad face and a little round belly,

That shook when he laughed, like a bowlful of jelly.

E was chubby and plump, a right jolly old elf,

And I laughed when I saw him, in spite of myself;

A wink of his eye and a twist of his head,

Soon gave me to know I had nothing to dread;

E spoke not a word, but went straight to his work,

And filled all the stockings; then turned with a jerk,

And laying his finger aside of his nose,

And giving a nod, up the chimney he rose;

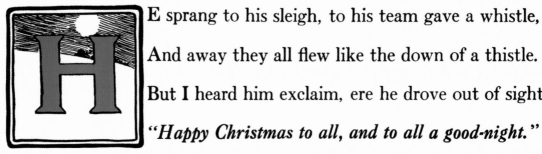E sprang to his sleigh, to his team gave a whistle,

And away they all flew like the down of a thistle.

But I heard him exclaim, ere he drove out of sight,

"Happy Christmas to all, and to all a good-night."